Sail in Trouble

Written by Jill Eggleton
Illustrated by Jim Storey

Sailor Sam ran up and down the boat.

"I'm not going to work today," he said.
"I'm going to play."

Sailor Sam went sliding
in the water.

The sailors saw Sailor Sam.
"We are working," they said.
"**You** have to help!"

"**No!**" said Sailor Sam.
"I'm playing today."

Sailor Sam saw a rope.
He went swinging
over the boat.

But he went too fast.
He fell into the water . . .

splash!

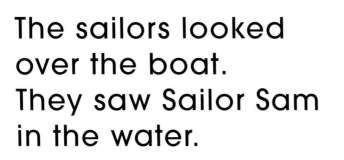

The sailors looked
over the boat.
They saw Sailor Sam
in the water.

"**Help me! Help me!**"
shouted Sailor Sam.
"Please help me up!"

The sailors put the rope down for Sailor Sam.

"Here is the rope," they said.
"But we can't get you up.
We have to work.
You can play with
the sharks."

Aaark!

The sailors went away.

"Come back!"
shouted Sailor Sam.
"Please get me up.
I see a shark!
I **will** help you!"

The sailors got Sailor Sam
onto the boat.
"Here is the mop,"
they said.
"You can work and
we will play."

A Story Sequence

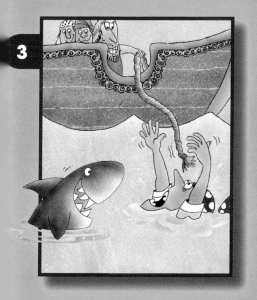

Guide Notes

Title: Sailor Sam in Trouble
Stage: Early (3) – Blue

Genre: Fiction
Approach: Guided Reading
Processes: Thinking Critically, Exploring Language, Processing Information
Written and Visual Focus: Story Sequence, Speech Bubbles
Word Count: 168

THINKING CRITICALLY
(sample questions)
- What do you think this story could be about?
- Focus on the title and discuss.
- Look at the cover. Why do you think Sailor Sam is throwing water on the sailor?
- Look at pages 2 and 3. What do you think the other sailors might be thinking about Sailor Sam?
- Look at pages 6 and 7. How do you know Sailor Sam was not very sensible?
- Look at pages 8 and 9. What do you think could happen to Sailor Sam if the sailors do not help him?
- Look at pages 12 and 13. What do you think made Sailor Sam change his mind about helping on the boat?
- Look at page 14. Why do you think the sailors said, "You can work and we will play."?

EXPLORING LANGUAGE

Terminology
Title, cover, illustrations, author, illustrator

Vocabulary
Interest words: sailors, rope, sliding, swinging, sharks, trouble
High-frequency words: fast, today, please, playing, back, play, ran
Positional words: in, down, up, over, into, onto

Print Conventions
Capital letter for sentence beginnings and names (**S**ailor **S**am), periods, commas, exclamation marks, quotation marks, ellipsis